D0998800

The
Raven
and
Other
Fairy Tales

The Raven and Other Fairy Tales

retold and illustrated by

Joan Balfour Payne

Hastings House, Publishers, New York

Contents

Published simultaneously in Canada by
Saunders, of Toronto, Ltd. Don Mills, Ontario

SBN: 8038-6310-1
Library of Congress Catalog Card Number: 72-81379
Printed in the United States of America

Fairy tales are the common heritage of the human race. The earliest ones were told between the very roots of the family tree of man and countless generations of story tellers have told and retold them with infinite variations. No children should leave childhood without having envisioned themselves in their magical roles of kings' sons and daughters, gifted with beauty and power over evil.

The following four stories I first retold and illustrated, without thought of publication, for the children of the Sewanee Kindergarten and Nursery School in Sewanee, Tennessee. Now I offer them, as a book, to all children who can delight in the magic, wit, and beauty of humanity's old tales.

Joan Balfour Payne
Sewanee, Tennessee
April, 1969

THERE WAS ONCE a queen who had a baby daughter. One night the child was so restless that the mother could not sleep. The queen rocked the baby and sang to her, but she would not be quieted. In the dawn, seeing a flight of ravens going over the castle, the queen cried,

"Oh, if only you were a raven and could fly away, then I might have peace!"

No sooner had the queen spoken than the child was turned into a raven and fluttered from her arms out the window. The queen wept bitterly for she had not meant what she said. But alas! the raven, her daughter, did not return!

Years passed and one day a young man, traveling through a forest, heard a voice cry, "I was born a king's daughter and have been bewitched, but you can set me free!"

The young man looked up and was amazed as he saw no one but a raven on a branch. He asked of the voice, "What shall I do?" And indeed it was the raven who spoke.

"Go deeper into the forest," said she, "and there you will find a little house in which sits an old, old woman. She will offer you meat and drink but you must touch nothing. Behind the house is a big stone. Go stand on it and wait for me. For three days, at noon, I will come to you. On the first day I will come in a chariot drawn by gazelles, on the second day in a chariot drawn by leopards, on the third day in a chariot drawn by lions. If you are sleeping when I come you will fail to set me free of my enchantment."

The young man promised to do all that she asked and went on his way. When he came to the little house he saw that it was made of feathers and an old, old woman, dressed all in feathers, was within. She came out and offered him food and drink. The young man was so hungry and thirsty that he forgot the raven's warning, and ate and drank. Then, as it was near noon, he went to stand on the stone and wait for the raven. Soon he felt so weary that he lay down and fell asleep.

When the raven came in the chariot drawn by gazelles she alighted and shook him, calling him sadly, but he would not awaken. The next day he vowed that he would take nothing that the old woman offered, and when she came to him with the bowl of meat and the horn of wine he refused.

But after a time the temptation was too great and he tasted both. Then he went to stand on the stone and wait for the raven. But again he became drowsy and lay down, and when the raven came in a chariot drawn by leopards, the young man was fast asleep. Try as she would, the raven could not awaken him.

On the third day, though the young man was determined not to touch what the old woman offered him, it all happened as before, and when the raven came for the last time in the chariot drawn by lions, he was again fast asleep.

Then the raven took from the chariot a loaf of bread, a haunch of meat, and a flask of wine. She laid these sadly by his side. Lastly, she drew a ring of gold from her claw and put it on his finger, saying,

"Farewell, it is all over and done. You might have broken the evil spell but now it is too late. Farewell, farewell!" And she drove away in the chariot.

When the young man awoke and saw these things he understood what had happened and was ashamed and grieved. Then and there he vowed to wander over the whole world until he found the enchanted raven again. Putting the bread, the meat, and the wine in his cloak, he set out. Of everyone he met he asked, "Have you seen or heard of the enchanted raven?" But no one could tell him of her.

Then, one night as he wandered through a wasteland, he saw a glimmer of light, and going to discover what it might be, he found that it came from a great cave in a cliff of red rock. While he stood there wondering, a huge shadow came between him and the light, and a giant stepped from the cave's mouth.

"I am very glad that you have come," said the giant. "It is a long time since I had anything to eat and you will make a very tasty supper."

"That may be," replied the young man, "but I don't like that idea at all! Besides, I have something here in my cloak

which will please you better." And he brought out the bread, the meat, and the wine, which, of course, were magic foods and constantly replenished themselves no matter how often he ate of them.

"Well, it was only for lack of something better that I wished to eat you," said the giant. So he and the young man sat down to eat together like old friends.

When they were done the young man asked the giant if he had ever heard of a raven who had been a king's daughter, and he told the giant his story. The giant replied that he had not but that he would look on his map that had marked upon it every strange and wondrous thing in all the world.

It was a very large map and it took them seven full days to examine every portion of it. But on the evening of the seventh day the giant exclaimed, "Behold! A thousand miles from here there is a mountain of glass. Every day at noon a door in its peak opens and a raven flies out crying, "Alas for me who was born a king's daughter!" Three times around the mountain this raven flies, then enters by the door and is seen no more until the following day."

The young man rejoiced, knowing that this must be his lost raven. He bade the giant farewell with many thanks and set out again on his journey. It took him many months but finally he came to the foot of the mountain of glass. It was the hour of noon and, looking up, he saw the door open and the raven fly out crying, "Alas for me who was born a king's daughter!" Three times around the peak she flew, then disappeared once more into the mountain.

The young man searched and searched but he could find no way up the smooth steep slopes of glass. He had to content himself with building a small hut at the foot of the mountain from which he could watch the raven each day.

One morning the young man was awakened by a terrible din and, going out, he found three robbers fighting among themselves. He persuaded them to stop long enough to explain that they were fighting over three things of great value—a stick that would open any door it knocked upon, a cloak that would make its owner invisible, and a horse that could go over any obstacle. They could not agree on how these treasures should be divided.

"Let me see these wondrous things and I will decide for you," said the young man, and the robbers agreed to do so. At this, he seized the stick, threw the cloak around him, and

leapt astride the horse which he put in a gallop straight up the slopes of the glass mountain.

When they reached the peak the young man beat upon the door with the magic stick. It opened immediately and he rode the magic horse into a vast hall of glass, at the end of which sat the raven in a golden cage.

"Turn back! Turn back, whoever enters here!" cried the raven, for she could see neither horse nor rider because of the magic cloak. "An evil sorcerer dwells in this place and if he comes now it will be the end of you!"

At that instant the sorcerer did indeed enter the hall, looking about him in a rage and muttering spells, but he, too, could see no one. The young man rode up to him and, flinging off the magic cloak, struck the sorcerer such a blow with the magic stick that he fell down dead.

Immediately the door of the golden cage swung open and the raven flew out. The young man reached up and caught her by the wing, and slipped the golden ring on her claw. Thereupon she changed from a bird into a princess so beautiful that he fell on his knees before her.

"Arise," cried the princess. She smiled and gave him her hand. "You have finally found me and broken the evil spell. Now, if you wish, I will be your wife." As she spoke, all around them the mountain of glass was shifting and changing its shape until they were standing together in a marvelous palace of crystal and gold.

So the young man married the princess and, in that land which had lain so long under the evil sorcerer's spell, they ruled together happily and wisely.

The Queen Bee

ONCE THERE WERE three king's sons who decided to go out into the world to see what could be seen.

On the first day they came upon a big ant hill whose tiny citizens were busily running to and fro storing up food and caring for their young. The two older brothers were all for kicking the ant hill down, but the youngest kept them from it, saying, "Let the ants alone. They have done you no harm." So the three princes passed by, leaving the ant hill to stand.

The second day they came to a lake on which a flock of ducks was swimming. The two older brothers would have shot the ducks for sport, but the youngest kept them from it, saying, "Leave the ducks alone. They have done you no harm." So the three king's sons passed by and left the ducks peacefully diving for water weeds.

On the third day they came on a great bee hive in a hollow tree. The bees were busily flying to and fro gathering flower nectar and feeding their queen. The two older brothers would have set fire to the hive and stolen the honey, but the younger brother kept them from it, saying, "Leave the bees alone. They have done you no harm." So the bee hive was saved.

After much wandering the princes came to a castle where stone horses were standing in the stable and stone men-at-arms were standing in the courtyard. The three brothers went through all the halls and apartments but saw no living thing, only stone servants and stone ladies and gentlemen standing here and there. They came to a splendid banquet hall where there was a great table laid with dishes of stone fruit and stone meats and bread. In the center of the table there was a stone book in which were written these words: "Any man who can accomplish the following tasks will set this castle free of its enchantment." And underneath were listed the three tasks.

The first one was to gather the thousand pearls that lay scattered under the moss in the nearby forest. If, by sunset of the day on which this task was begun, one single pearl was missing, he who had looked for them would be turned to stone.

The next morning the eldest brother went into the forest, boasting that he would gather the pearls quite easily. But at sunset he did not return.

The morning after that the middle brother went into the forest and there he found the elder turned to stone with sev-

eral hundred pearls around his feet. These the middle brother gathered up, and then he set about looking for the rest, confident that he would find them all. But at sunset of that day he did not return.

The following morning the youngest brother went into the forest and saw his two brothers turned to stone, with the pearls that they had found all scattered at their feet. He was so grieved that he sat down to weep and mourn and never noticed how the hours passed. But when the sun was low in the sky, a tiny voice spoke to him, saying,

"Here, O king's youngest, here are the thousand pearls. You saved our lives and our city from the cruelty of your thoughtless brothers, and now we repay the debt!"

Looking down, the young prince saw a thousand ants, each holding a pearl, and there was just time for the pearls to be dropped into his purse before the sun set. Then, with many thanks to the ants and a sad farewell to his brothers, he returned to the castle.

The second task was to bring up from the bottom of the castle moat the golden key that would open the door to the castle tower. If it was not found by sunset the seeker would be turned to stone.

The young prince stripped to the waist and dove into the water again and again, but he could not find the key. He was ready to give up with weariness when a flock of ducks came flying over and settled on the moat with much quacking. They all began to dive and the prince thought that they were only feeding. But just before sunset the leader swam up to the exhausted prince and laid a golden key at his feet, saying,

"Here, O king's youngest, is the golden key. You saved me and my flock from the cruelty of your thoughtless brothers and now we repay our debt!" The young prince was delighted and thanked the ducks warmly.

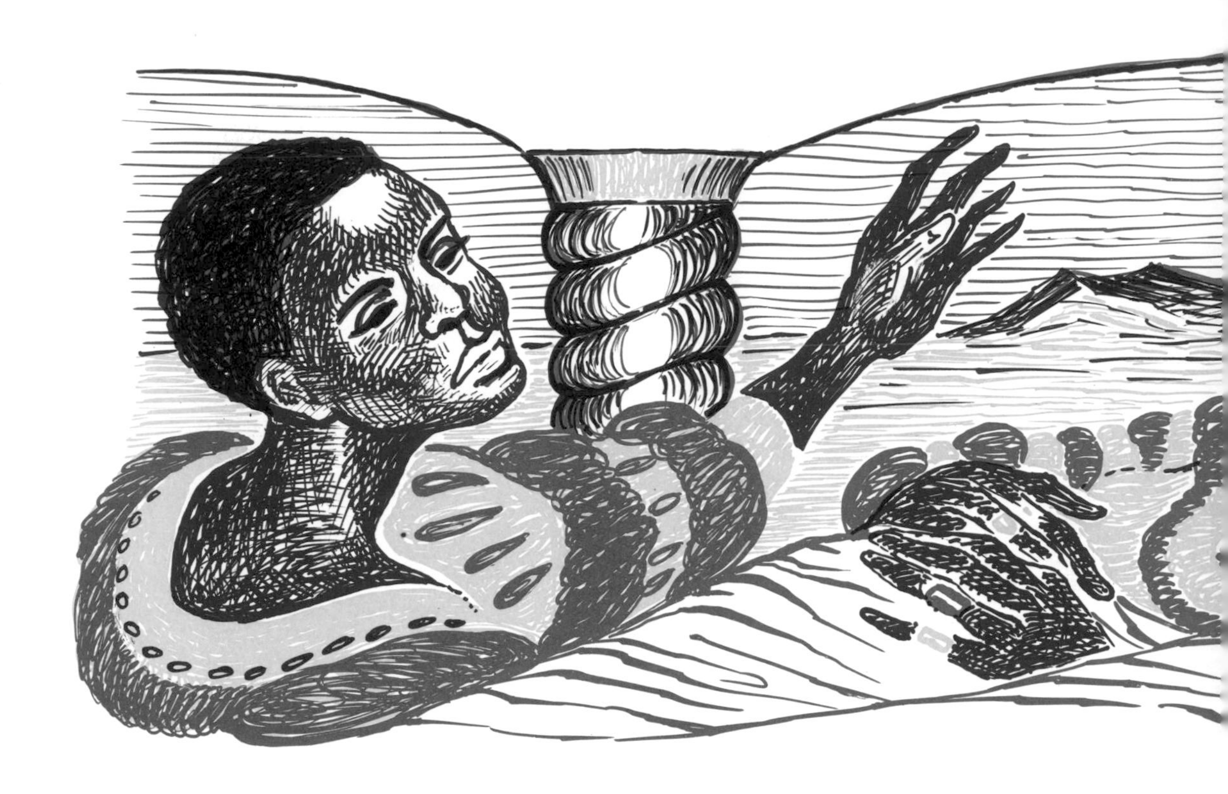

Then he entered the castle and unlocked the tower door. Inside the tower was a flight of stairs which he followed upward to a richly furnished chamber where three lovely princesses lay sleeping. The young prince stood gazing at them, certain that he had never before seen such beauty, and he remembered the third task that he must accomplish. This was to guess which princess had eaten the sweetest of sweetmeats before falling asleep. As the young prince could think of no way to find the answer except by asking, he tried to awaken them. He spoke to them, shook them, and clapped his hands loudly, but the three beauties did not even stir.

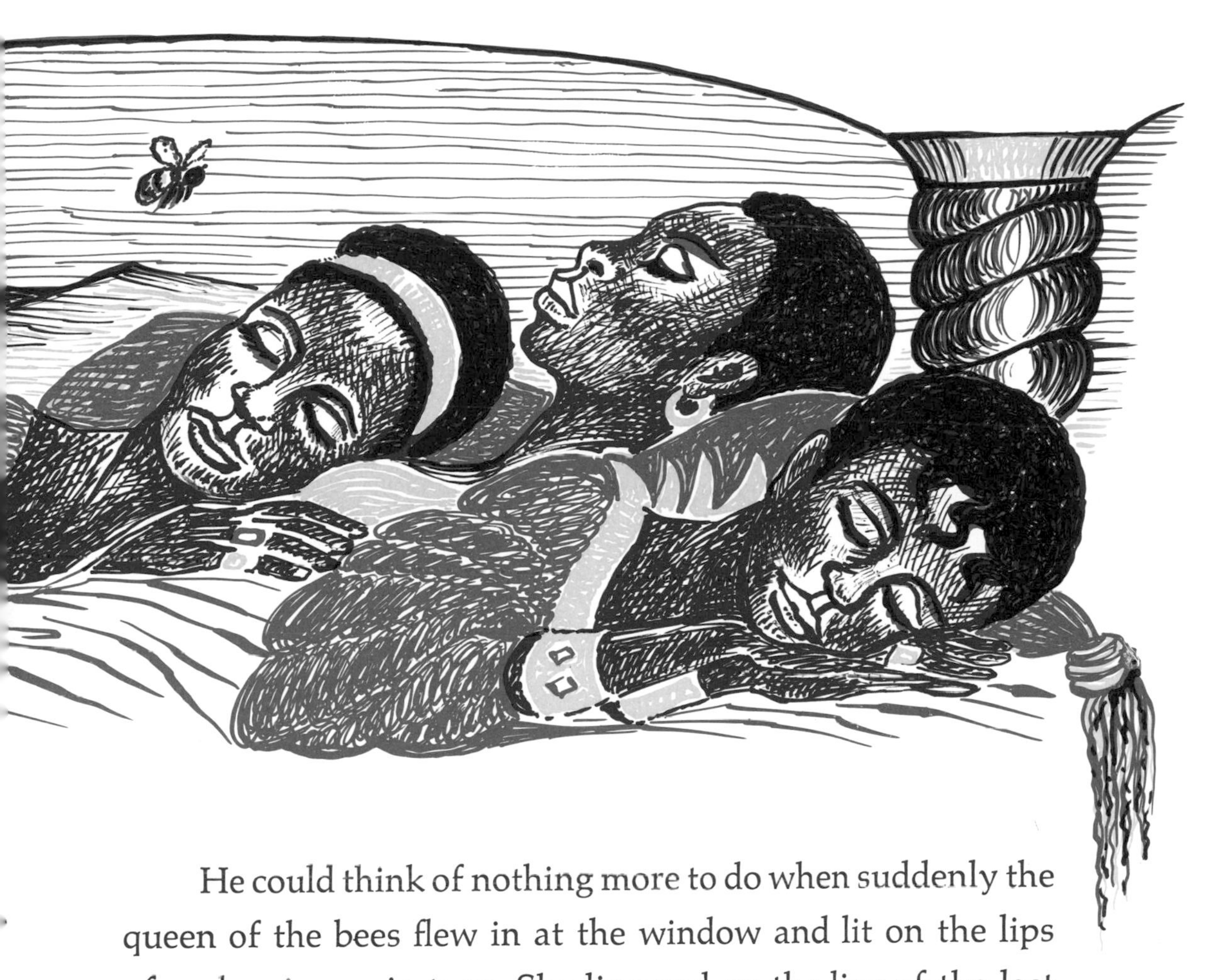

He could think of nothing more to do when suddenly the queen of the bees flew in at the window and lit on the lips of each princess in turn. She lingered on the lips of the last and most beautiful of the three, saying,

"Here, O king's youngest, is the princess who has eaten the sweetest of sweetmeats. You once saved me and my hive from the cruelty of your thoughtless brothers, and now I repay the debt!"

The young prince thanked the queen bee warmly, then he bent and kissed the loveliest princess and at that moment the three tasks were accomplished. The three princesses woke up and the castle came to life again with horses neighing in the stables, men-at-arms walking the watch, and servants scurrying to and fro. Even the prince's two older brothers were released from their enchantment and came in from the forest.

In time the youngest prince and the loveliest princess were married, and she proved to be not only beautiful but sweet-tempered as well. They lived very happily ever after.

The two older brothers married the two other princesses, who were certainly pretty enough but who turned out to be great scolds and made their husbands' lives quite miserable! Life is sometimes like that.

THERE WAS ONCE a village girl called Beauty because she was so handsome. Her eyes were like black diamonds, her hair grew in glossy curls as black as a raven's wing, and her skin was like dark polished wood. She was clever as well, and could bake, brew, spin, and weave better than all the other maidens. She was also kindhearted.

One day three old women came to the village. One had fiery red eyes, and a great hump on her back, another had enormous feet and bandy legs, and the third had a huge pendulous lip and great flat fingers. They were so ugly that everyone was afraid of them and ran indoors to hide. But Beauty, seeing only that they were aged and weary, offered them a place to rest and bowls of fresh milk. The three old women rested and drank but said never a word, and presently they went on their way with no thanks at all to Beauty.

Beauty's mother was a foolish and boastful woman. It was not enough for her that her daughter was so handsome and clever; she had to make up silly stories. One day at the village well she told the other women that Beauty could spin and weave fine silk from thistledown, bake fine bread from thistle stalks, and make fine wine from thistle juice. A messenger of the queen, who was passing through the village, heard her and went straight to his mistress with the story.

The old queen thought, "Aha! if the tale is true what a fine wife for my son this Beauty will be!" She sent for Beauty

and her mother to learn if the girl really could do such wonders with thistles. The silly mother dared not say she had lied for fear of punishment and poor Beauty dared not tell the truth for her mother's sake. So the queen said that she would have to see these wonders for herself, and she ordered that Beauty be locked in a room filled with thistles and all the things needed for spinning, weaving, baking, and wine making. If, at the end of three days, Beauty had made good use of the thistles, she would marry the queen's only son. But if she could not do as her mother had boasted, both she and her mother would be sorely punished.

Poor Beauty was greatly troubled, but since she was a clever and good-natured girl, she tried her best. She stripped and kneaded the harsh thistles until her hands bled, but could find no way to bake or spin or weave them. Then she trod out the harsh juices with her bare feet until she could scarcely stand for the pain, but the juices remained bitter and undrinkable.

On the third day Beauty gave up in despair and lay down with her face to the wall. Presently, to her great surprise, she smelled fine bread baking and fine wine making, and she heard the sounds of thread being twisted on a spindle and woven on a loom. She looked up and saw there in the chamber—although the door was still locked—the three ugly old women whom she had once befriended. They spoke not a word, but worked away until, at the day's end, every thistle had been used and there was a vat of fine wine, twenty loaves of white bread, and a bolt of fine silk cloth.

"Now, Beauty," said the ugliest of the three, "you must say nothing about this to anyone. It is our thanks for your kindness. But one thing you must surely do if you wish your married life to run smoothly. On the day that you marry the prince we will appear at the wedding feast and you must say that we are your godmothers. Then you must seat us at the bride's table with you and your bridegroom. Do not forget!"

Beauty promised and, although she could not tell how they managed it, the three old women disappeared from the room. When the queen came to unlock the door and saw that Beauty had performed the impossible task, she kissed the clever girl and called for the wedding to be arranged at once.

So Beauty was married to the prince amid great pomp and splendor, and she and her bridegroom were very pleased with each other. Beauty's only fear was that she might again be expected to work wonders with thistles and she could not imagine what she would do then! But in the midst of the feast the three ugly old women arrived. The other wedding guests wondered at them and the guards would have driven them away, but Beauty went to them, smiling a welcome, and led them to seats between herself and the prince, saying to all, "These are my dear godmothers to whom I owe all that I am!"

Now the prince thought that the three old women were quite dreadful, but, because he was a true prince and because he wished to please his new bride, he did his best to be agreeable and talk with them.

"You have a clever girl for a wife," said the one who had a great hump on her back and fiery red eyes. "I taught her to bake and I am the best baker in the world as you can tell from my hump and my red eyes that come from bending over the dough and peering into the oven. Beauty will be as good as I if she keeps on."

"Yes, indeed," said the one who had enormous feet and bandy legs. "I taught her to make wine and I am the best wine-maker in the world as you can tell from my feet and legs that have been treading out juices all these years. Beauty will be as good as I if only she keeps on."

"And I taught her to spin and weave," added the third,

who had the huge pendulous lower lip and great flattened fingers. "I am the best spinner and weaver in the world as you can tell from my lip on which I wet the thread and my fingers that twist it. Beauty will be as good as I if only she keeps on."

"Mercy!" thought the prince, "my beautiful bride must not be allowed to do any more work lest she turn into such a creature as one of these!"

So Beauty was never again asked to spin or weave or bake or make wine, and no one ever knew that she really could not make bread and wine and silk cloth out of thistles. She was clever and beautiful, though, and she and the prince lived long and happily together.

THERE WAS ONCE an old countryman who had twelve sons. They were all good lads but the youngest was a wanderer. Once day he returned home after a long journey to find that his father had died and his brothers had divided up the inheritance between themselves, leaving him nothing.

"We thought that you were dead also, you were away so long," they told him, "but there are twelve old mares out on the hills that have not been divided. You may have those."

The young man went out on the hills to look at his share and found that each mare had a new foal at her side. They were nice-looking foals, but one, a dappled colt, was especially big and handsome. To his amazement, the dappled colt spoke to him, saying, "Sell all the other foals so that I may have all the mares' milk and in a year's time you will have a truly fine inheritance!"

The young man did as the colt bid him and then went off wandering again. When he returned the following year the mares had new foals at their sides but the dappled colt had grown to be the largest and finest yearling anyone had ever seen. Again the colt bid him sell the new foals and he did so. After three years of this procedure the colt had become such a huge and splendid horse that his equal had never been seen anywhere and the young man called him Dapplegrim.

"Give the twelve mares back to your brothers now," said Dapplegrim, "for I am all that you will ever need. In a cave there in the rocks you will find a saddle and bridle to fit me. Put them on me and let us be gone."

The young man found the saddle and bridle as he was told. They were wonderfully made of tooled leather with golden fittings, and so heavy that the young man had some trouble in saddling and bridling the great horse. But at last he mounted up and he and Dapplegrim were a splendid sight indeed. The eleven brothers watched in amazement as they galloped away.

In time Dapplegrim and his master came to a castle where lived a young enchantress so beautiful that kings and princes and noblemen wanted to marry her, but she would have none of them. "I will marry the man who can cut down the hill outside my eastern window so that I may see the golden face of my brother, the sun, as he rises in the morning," said she.

"Get a blacksmith to hammer me out four shoes from four hundred pounds of iron," Dapplegrim told his master who had immediately fallen in love with the enchantress. So the young man went out and bought the iron and found a blacksmith to do the job. When the great horse was thus shod with a hundred-pound shoe on each hoof, the young man mounted up and rode to the eastern wall of the castle. There Dapplegrim made three mighty leaps and the hill sank down to a level plain beneath him!

"That's nicely done," said the enchantress coolly. "Yet I will only marry the man who can root up the great thorn tree

that covers the western wall of my castle so that I may see the silver face of my sister, the evening star, as she swings in the western sky!"

The thorn tree was a thousand years old and so tough that no ax could hew it. But Dapplegrim told his master, "Bid the smith forge from six hundred pounds of iron a collar and a chain with a hook on the end." When that was done, with the collar around his neck, the hook around the thorn tree, and the young man in the saddle, Dapplegrim made three mighty bounds and tore the thorn's great roots out of the earth.

"Well, that's nicely done indeed," said the enchantress coolly, but she was secretly pleased for she liked the young man and his powerful horse. "Now I will turn myself twice into a strange form and you must discover what I am!" And she instantly disappeared.

The young man despaired for he had no way of knowing what form she had chosen. But Dapplegrim said, "Take your bow and arrow and go aim at the wild black swan that floats on the lake there."

The young man did so and the swan cried, "Do not loose the arrow—it is I!" And indeed it was the enchantress. Again she changed her form and Dapplegrim said, "Go into the kitchen where the new-baked loaves are cooling. Take up a sharp knife and pretend that you are going to slice the loaf with the darkest crust."

The young man did so and the loaf cried, "Do not cut—it is I!" And it was the enchantress who then said, "You are clever indeed and I will marry you gladly, but I cannot ride to my wedding on a lesser horse than yours. Bring me a match for Dapplegrim and we will wed immediately!"

When Dapplegrim heard this he sighed deeply and hung his great head against his master's breast. "Alas!" he said, "I know of only one match for me between Heaven and Hell, and he belongs to your enchantress's kinsmen, the Winds! The other tasks were nothing, but to take him may mean my death. Yet I will do what I can. Go slaughter twelve oxen and skin them. Have their hides sewn together and studded all over with iron spikes. Then get twelve sacks of grain and a great barrel of tar."

The young man hastened to do all these things and when they were done, Dapplegrim said, "Now saddle and bridle me. In front of the saddle hang the iron-studded hides and the barrel of tar. Behind the saddle hang the twelve ox carcasses and the twelve sacks of grain. Then bid your enchantress farewell and mount up, for we must be on our way!"

Thus they set out and on the twelfth day of their journey Dapplegrim asked, "Do you hear anything?" and his master answered, "Yes, I hear a great rushing and crying in the air afar off, and it chills my heart!"

Dapplegrim said, "That is all the birds in the world sent to stop us. But reach behind you and slash open the twelve sacks so that the grain runs out onto the ground. The birds will stop to fight over it and forget about us." Then the sky grew black with birds so that it seemed like night, but the young man did as he was bid and everything happened as Dapplegrim said it would.

On the twelfth day after that Dapplegrim asked again, "Do you hear anything?" His master answered, "I hear a great crashing and a running and a roaring afar off and it chills my heart!".

Dapplegrim replied, "That is all the wild beasts in the world sent to stop us. But reach behind you and cut loose the twelve ox carcasses. The wild beasts will stop to fight over them and will forget about us." The young man did as he was bid and it all happened as Dapplegrim said.

On the twelfth day thereafter Dapplegrim asked once more, "Do you hear anything?" and his master replied, "I hear a whinnying afar off like that of a foal." But when they had gone some distance further the young man said, "Now I hear a neighing like that of a full-grown horse close at hand!"

They had come to a vast plain where no trees or grass grew. Only a few jagged rocks stood up here and there. "Dismount," said Dapplegrim, "and take off my saddle and bridle. Hide yourself behind one of those rocks, but be sure to

keep my bridle ready in your hand. Only first open the barrel of tar and spill it out. Then throw over me the iron-studded oxhides."

The young man did this and the tar spilled out and spread until it covered a large area of the plain. "Here we will fight," said Dapplegrim, "and the sparks from our iron shoes will set the field of tar on fire. If at any time the flames gutter and go out, take to your heels and do not look back for I will have died and there will be no help for you. But if the flames burn high and you see my adversary's knees touch the ground, step out boldly and throw my bridle over his head and the day will be ours!"

When he had covered Dapplegrim with the ox hides, the young man hid himself behind a rock. Presently there was a fierce neighing and a thunder of hooves, and an enormous horse appeared. In size he was like Dapplegrim but he was reddish brown in color whereas Dapplegrim was grey. The two horses trumpeted and reared, clashed and fought until

the sparks from their iron shoes set the field of tar afire. This fire burned sometimes high and sometimes low as the two horses plunged and struck. Wherever Dapplegrim bit, his teeth sank in but the other horse could get no hold on the iron-studded ox hides.

For twelve days and nights they fought ceaselessly. Fi-

nally Dapplegrim forced his adversary onto his knees while the flames leaped high around them. Then the young man rushed in and flung the bridle over the other horse's head and he immediately became as docile as a new lamb. The young man mounted up and, with Dapplegrim cantering alongside, he rode his prize back to the castle of the enchantress.

The young man and the enchantress were married soon after that and they rode to their wedding in great splendor, she in cloth-of-silver on the brown horse, he in cloth-of-gold on Dapplegrim. Their life together was a very happy one.

After a year's time, her kinsmen, the Winds, came for their horse and rode him home one night that was long remembered by all who heard them go, for their passage was like a terrible storm over land and sea.

But Dapplegrim stayed on with his master until the end of his days.

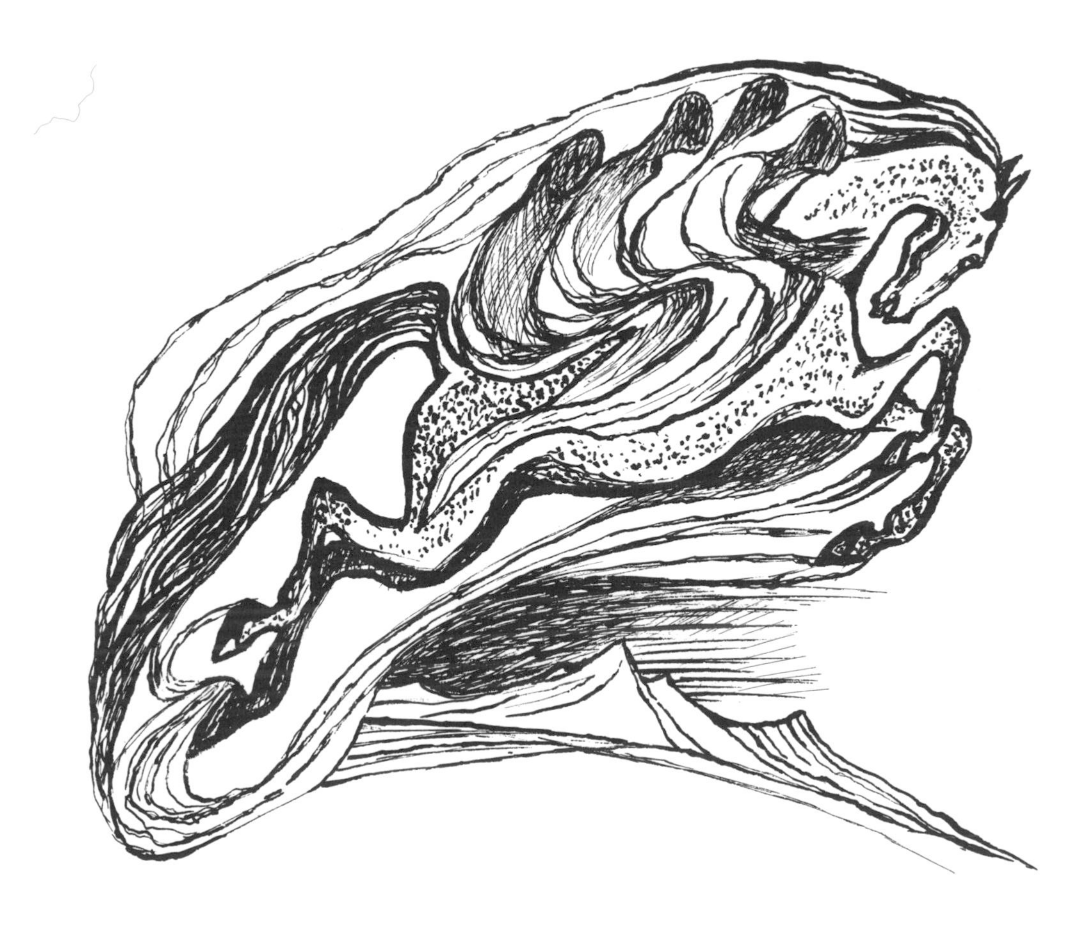

About Joan Balfour Payne

This author-artist first attained fame in 1952 as illustrator of *The Stable That Stayed* (Ariel Books), written by her mother, Josephine Balfour Payne. This was one of the Honor Books in the *New York Herald Tribune* Spring Book Festival, as was their next work, *The Journey of Josiah Talltatters* (Ariel Books). Then Joan stepped off on her own and both wrote and illustrated *The Piebald Princess* (Ariel Books). It was also a Spring Festival Honor Book.

Since then Joan has written and illustrated seven more picture books, including this one.

Mrs. Dicks was born in Natchez, Mississippi and is one of the few author-illustrators of children's books coming from this state. She attended the Northrop Collegiate School for Girls in Minneapolis and studied art under Gustav Krollman at the Minneapolis Institute of Art. At present she and her husband and their four children live in Sewanee, Tennessee. Dr. Dicks is professor of physics at the University of Tennessee Space Institute.

OTHER PICTURE BOOKS

Written and Illustrated by

JOAN BALFOUR PAYNE

PANGUR BAN

"A ninth-century Gaelic poem is the inspiration for an original story in folktale style. A daring Irish cat in search of a nobler way of life than catching mice and chasing birds achieves his goal in a triumphant battle with Maev, Queen of the Fairy People. The illustrations and distinguished prose dramatically convey the humor, vigor and Celtic flavor of this simple tale." — *American Library Association Booklist.*

THE LEPRECHAUN OF BAYOU LUCE

"Surely only one leprechaun has ever found his way from Ireland to the banks of the Mississippi River and Joss Turnipseed happens to meet him! . . . A charming tale of nonsense and fantasy . . . The humor and originality of both text and pictures make this a good read aloud story guaranteed to tickle the funny bone of young and old."— *Saturday Review*

GENERAL BILLYCOCK'S PIGS

"General Billycock had a terrible temper. When the pigs came to his Tennessee fields — and stayed — he became sick with rage. . . . How his 9-year-old daughter Betsy and a neighbor boy purged the general of his bad temper makes a genuinely exciting story. Even more to the author's credit, she has evoked a brilliant panorama of life in early Tennessee. Here too are humor, pathos, suspense and most important, very real people. A fine book."— *The New York Times Book Review*

MAGNIFICENT MILO

"Joan Balfour Payne has a particular flare. Here we have Milo, a young centaur, whose excursion into the world of men makes for very entertaining text and illustrations. 8- and 10-year-olds will love it." — *Library Journal.* "One has come to expect something uncommon in each book from this author-artist, and this is no disappointment . . . fresh, amusing and sketched with humorous detail." — *The Horn Book.*